SANDMARE

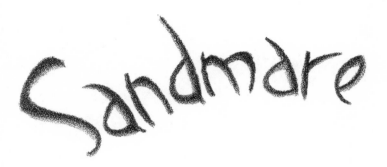

Sandmare

HELEN COOPER
ILLUSTRATED BY TED DEWAN

Farrar Straus Giroux · New York

First published in Great Britain by Young Corgi. Corgi Books are published
by Transworld Publishers, a division of the Random House Group Ltd
Printed in the United States of America
First American edition, 2003
1   3   5   7   9   10   8   6   4   2

Library of Congress Cataloging-in-Publication Data
Cooper, Helen (Helen F.)
    Sandmare / Helen Cooper ; pictures by Ted Dewan.— 1st American ed.
        p.   cm.
    Summary: A powerful wish allows the horse that Polly and her father draw
in the beach sand to come to life and pursue her dream of reaching the stars.
    ISBN 0-374-36406-0
    [1. Wishes—Fiction.   2. Horses—Fiction.   3. Beaches—Fiction.
4. Drawing—Fiction.   5. Persistence—Fiction.]   I. Dewan, Ted, ill.   II. Title.

PZ7.C78555 San 2003
[Fic]—dc21

                                                                2002021606

FOR CORY AND ADDY

CONTENTS

SANDMARE

THE SAND HORSE

"Draw a horse," said Polly.

Dad made a face. Horses are hard to draw.

"Please," Polly begged. The sand was just right for drawing on.

Dad reached for a piece of shell.

He used it to draw some
sharp, pointy lines. They
were the ears.

Next he drew a gentle
curved line toward the nose.
Then the line flicked
around the mouth, curved
up under the chin, and
glided down to make the
horse's neck.

"I need an eye," he called.

Polly was ready.
She held out a round
brown pebble.

"Perfect." Dad smiled.
He looked hard at the
drawing. Then he popped
the pebble right where the
eye should be.

Now the horse was alive. Drawings often come to life once the eyes are in the right place. These drawings can't usually move. But sometimes they can think. This horse could. And it knew that it was a special drawing, even when it was only halfway done.

"That back leg's wrong," said Polly.

"I know," sighed Dad. "I can't do legs."

In the end he let Polly cover most of the back leg with a thick swishy tail. They couldn't hide the front legs, so he only drew one. It didn't look too bad. And the horse didn't mind. It was happy with two legs.

Polly drew in a mane with her finger. "Is it a she horse?"

"A mare?" said Dad. "Could be."

"Yes, I am a mare," whispered the horse so quietly that no one heard.

"I think she's fantastic," said Polly. "It's sad that the waves will wash her away when the tide comes in."

Dad took some chicken out of the picnic basket.

"When will the waves come in?" asked Polly, munching.

"Just after sunset," said Dad, holding out the wishbone.

"So I have the rest of the afternoon," murmured the Sandmare to herself. "Well, that's not so bad . . . But I wish I weren't trapped in the sand."

SNAP went the wishbone.

Polly waved the long end. "I wish that the Sandmare could run free."

They peered down at the Sandmare. Dad rubbed Polly's hair.

"That sort of wish doesn't often come true," he said, smiling.

Maybe not often! But Polly and the Sandmare had wished at the same time, so the wish was very strong.

THE WISH

The picnic was packed away, and Polly had put on her shoes. She leaned over and whispered, "Good luck," into the Sandmare's ear.

Then she was gone.

"I hope the wish works," thought the Sandmare. She was sure she could feel it quivering and crackling around her. "But it had better be soon. Those waves are coming nearer."

The sun had noticed the wish as it toasted the beach with its oven breath. Now that the beach was empty, it called down to the sea, "I think we ought to give that horse drawing a chance."

"Why bother?" the sea sighed. "I've swallowed whole centuries of sand drawings. That one will be mine in the end, just like the rest."

"And yet," whispered the beach drowsily, "there will still be sand left, after you've swallowed it up. The Sandmare is my child."

"The Sandmare wants to escape from both of you," the sun reminded them.

"Where could she escape to?" moaned the sea. "There is nowhere safe for a creature like that."

"Perhaps if she ran very far . . ." whispered the beach.

"Very far," agreed the sun. "There is some hope . . . but only if the Sandmare tries her hardest and doesn't give up."

The sea was bored. "I'll give the sand creature one night to try," it hissed.

The beach shrugged beneath the Sandmare. "One night, then," it rumbled. "She'll be back to sand in the morning."

"I bet she doesn't even leave the beach," gurgled the sea.

"I'll show them," thought the Sandmare. She struggled to shake herself free. Nothing happened. She was still stuck fast. "What shall I do?" She stared up at the sun, hoping for help. None came. The sun had slipped behind a cloud.

A scruffy long-nosed dog, out for his evening walk, pattered along the beach.

 He stopped to snuffle around the Sandmare. If you have ever been flat on your back with a wet dog snuffling around you (a dog you have never met), then you will know how the Sandmare felt. She had to stare up at the dog's muddy tummy. She had to feel the dog's damp, sniffling nose, and smell the doggy breath. Then the dog lifted up his back leg and . . .

"DON'T!" screamed the Sandmare.

The dog leaped sideways. "I beg your pardon," he barked. "I was just . . . um . . ."

"Well, do it somewhere else," snorted the Sandmare.

The dog disappeared behind a rock. Then he came back, wagging his tail.

"You talked," he woofed. "You humphed, and you shouted, and your nose moved. Do it again."

The Sandmare twitched her nostrils.

"See!" yapped the dog, jumping up and down. "See."

The Sandmare found she could frown. "There was a wish," she said. "I think it must be working a bit."

"Is a bit enough?" panted the dog. "Can you get up now? Those waves are pretty close."

The Sandmare peeped at the sea from the corner of her pebble eye. The waves had almost reached her tail, yet she still couldn't budge.

The dog trotted around her. "Try harder."

Sandmare strained as hard as she could. Her muscles shook, her tail swished . . . But that was all.

"I'll wish, too." The dog squeezed his eyes shut.

And now the Sandmare found that she could lift her head . . . But what was the use of that without the rest of her? The effort was making her tremble all over. The beach seemed to throb around the part of her still in the sand.

"Come *on*," woofed the dog. "The water's almost touching you."

"I'm trying so hard that it's making me shake," neighed the Sandmare.

The dog pricked up his ears. "You're not shaking!" he barked in alarm. "That's the beach ponies. They gallop this way at sunset. You've got to move!"

The Sandmare could hear the thudding, too.

"They won't see you," panted the dog. "Quick! You'll be trampled. I'm out of here." And with that he bolted away down the beach.

"Now or never!" The Sandmare struggled frantically.

She could hear the ponies blowing on the sand.

She could see the next wave splashing toward her, the wave that would wash away her tail.

And at that second, a last spindle spike of orange sunlight winked through

the clouds and touched her hooves. Up
she bounded in a shower of sand,
shaking her mane, and whisking her tail
from the water.

THE BEACH PONIES

You can imagine how wonderful it was for the Sandmare when she ran for the first time—all that cool sunset air whooshing through her mane, while the ground sped away beneath her hooves.

"Catch the stars!" whinnied the beach ponies as the evening star appeared in the sky.

"Yes! Catch the stars," answered the Sandmare, straining ahead. She joined the beach ponies in their wild gallop and felt that she could race forever.

Of course, she didn't gallop like the flesh-and-blood ponies. Don't forget she only had two legs. She had to find her own way of moving. Sometimes she rocked from one leg to the other, front to back to front again, like a rocking horse. Sometimes she moved her two legs in, then out, then in again, like a pair of scissors. Best of all, she bounced on both legs at once like a spring lamb. But not too high. There was a man riding one of the ponies way behind them. He hadn't seen the Sandmare so far, and she wanted it to stay that way.

Now the man called out to the ponies, "Steady there." To the Sandmare's confusion, the ponies slowed to a trot and went through a gate, into a scruffy field.

Luckily, the man must have wanted his supper. He shut the gate and walked away without noticing the Sandmare. The Sandmare held her breath until he had gone.

Then she burst out, "We didn't catch the stars."

The ponies all turned around and stared at the Sandmare. The lead pony was called Anchor because of the shape of the splotch on his tummy. "It's just a game," he snorted. "We never really catch the stars. They're too far away."

"But I need to go somewhere far away," said the Sandmare. "If I'm still here in the morning, I'll turn back into sand."

The beach ponies sucked air through

their teeth. "You won't get very far in one night," explained Anchor. "You're not very fast, you know."

"I have to try," whinnied the Sandmare.

"How far do you need to go?" neighed a gray pony called Silver.

The Sandmare was flustered now. "I don't know, just far . . . maybe as far as the stars."

"You can't possibly," snorted Silver. "The church clock just struck six. There's only eleven hours before morning."

The other ponies stamped their feet and looked embarrassed. Then an old black pony called Velvet lifted her head from the scrubby grass. "Isn't there someone else who might help you?" she asked.

"There was a girl," said the Sandmare. "She was nice. She drew my tail."

"Then she must be quite clever," said Velvet. "Why don't you ask her?"

"There you are," neighed Anchor. "She made you. She should know what to do."

"But you've got to find her first," warned Silver.

"The golden horses might know where she is," whinnied a young black pony.

"They're supposed to be very wise," agreed Velvet.

20

"Look to the end of the beach," said Anchor. "Do you see the Shining City stretching out onto the water? You'll find them there, in a beautiful round temple."

"But you mustn't look them in the eye," said Velvet. "Always look down. It's bad to look them in the eye."

"Why?" asked the Sandmare.

There was silence for a moment.

"We don't know. We've never seen them," said Anchor. "But when we were foals we were always told—"

"It's polite," harrumphed Velvet. "It's the right way to talk to them. Just wait until the people have gone home. Then see what the golden horses have to say."

"And be careful," warned Anchor. "They may not be quite safe."

THE MERRY-GO-ROUND HORSES

More stars twinkled as the Sandmare dashed along the beach. "They don't look that far away," she thought. "I bet I could reach them right now. Those ponies gave up far too easily."

So she tried. She rocked, and she scissored, and she bounced across the beach, and stretched upward until she was exhausted. But the stars seemed as far away as ever. And she was even more disappointed when she looked over at the "Shining City."

She could see now that the lights only shone from a seaside pier. The kind of pier with bumper cars, and a striped giant slide, and scruffy pink-and-blue booths selling cotton candy and burgers. There was no sign of a golden temple. Gloomily she rested in the shadows of the steps and wondered what to do next.

Then she spotted the splendid merry-go-round with its glittering horses. "Maybe that's what the beach ponies meant," she whispered.

Now she could hardly wait for the
people on the pier to go home. But they
didn't for ages. It was nine o'clock
when the music stopped, and
children finished
swinging on the huge
plastic gorilla.

At half-past
nine the lights
went out, leaving
only one dim red
bulb flashing atop
the giant slide.

The Sandmare
crept forward, and red
shadows shimmered in the
mirrors of the merry-go-round.

"No need to be scared," she told
herself. "It's only that spooky red light."
She gave a little bow toward the red-
and-gold horses and, carefully looking
away from their eyes, she blurted out,
"Excuse me . . ."

"We know why you came," sang an eerie wooden voice.

A whole chorus of others joined in, all chanting together, "We know you. We know everyone on our beach."

The Sandmare shuffled her feet.

It's hard not to look up when you're waiting for someone to speak. She glanced sideways at them. Which one had spoken first? The one with the jeweled crown?

"C-could you tell me where to find the girl who helped make me?" she stammered. (She only looked up as far as its spangled neck.)

"The child can't help you." (It was the one with the crown who spoke.)

Then the whole ghostly horse choir joined in, chanting, "You belong to the beach and the sea. Go back where you belong, Sandmare." And slowly, as if blown by the wind, the merry-go-round began to circle.

"Please," called the Sandmare. "The little girl might be able to help me escape from here."

"Why would you want to leave?" they sang.

"Come closer," called the crowned horse. "Look at the sea."

The Sandmare crept forward. There was a good view from the pier.

"Can you see them?" hummed the

crowned horse. "Can you see the white horses dancing on the waves?"

"I can see froth," the Sandmare said, frowning.

"Froth?" he said gravely. "Do you think you are the only sand horse we have seen?"

"There have been many," the horse choir joined in.

"All those white horses were once drawings, too," droned the crowned horse. "Go back to the beach, Sandmare. Let the waves take you. You should be with the other white horses of the sea."

"Must I?" the Sandmare wondered. The merry-go-round spun faster now. It made her feel dizzy.

Suddenly a rich voice boomed out from behind the merry-go-round.

"Sorry to interrupt. But if you ask me, 'white horse' is just a fancy name for foam on the waves."

The Sandmare tried to see who had spoken. "I don't want to be foam," she whinnied.

"Quiet," commanded the crowned horse. 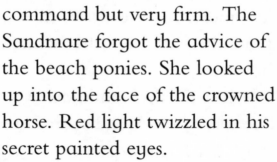 It was a soft, steady sort of command but very firm. The Sandmare forgot the advice of the beach ponies. She looked up into the face of the crowned horse. Red light twizzled in his secret painted eyes.

Immediately the Sandmare felt heavy, and weary, and confused.

The church clock struck ten.

"Look away," she thought. She couldn't.

"Go back to the sea," lulled the whirling horse choir.

"Look away," she told herself again.

It grew colder. A night wind rattled the shutters of the burger booth, swung the strings of lightbulbs, and clanked the pleasure boats against the pier.

Eleven o'clock struck . . . then twelve . . . Still the Sandmare gazed on, in a trance.

"Maybe I should go back to the beach," she murmured.

The rich mystery voice spoke urgently. "Sandmare, are you

still there? You shouldn't be listening to those wooden-heads. They don't know as much as they make out. It's time you spoke to someone else."

"I wanted to speak to that little girl," exploded the Sandmare.

"Children know nothing," snickered the horses gently through their painted teeth.

"I'd still like to find Polly," muttered the Sandmare.

"Polly! Why didn't you say so? I see

her all the time," called the mystery voice. "Come on, now. You're strong. Get out of there while you still can."

"Go to the sea," sang the horses.

But the Sandmare had woken up. "Not until I have to," she decided. She closed her eyes tight, shut off her ears, and sprang sideways and away before they could call her back.

THE GLASS HORSE

"Thank goodness," said the voice.

The Sandmare opened her eyes. She was standing in front of the plastic gorilla.

"Ask *me* about Polly," he boomed. "I know all about her. She never bothers with that bunch of wooden idiots. One of 'em threw her off when she was little. I looked after her. Now she comes and pats me every day . . . after she's visited the glass horse."

"Where can I find her, then?" asked the Sandmare.

The gorilla scratched his ear. "Find

her? Oh, I don't know where you could find her . . . But she'll be here this afternoon. Just wait here with me."

The Sandmare felt like crying. "I can't wait," she whinnied. "Haven't you any idea where she lives?"

The gorilla pulled at his eyebrow. "The glass horse might know. Polly talks about him. He's in a shop. Go straight across the road, and it's on your left. You could ask him."

The Sandmare thanked the gorilla. "I'll go there right now," she neighed.

Through the window, the Sandmare could see that the shop was cluttered with hats and cookie tins, tangled together with a dressmaker's dummy, two birdcages, a stuffed fox, and a jar full of peacock feathers. The glass horse was on a table between a mermaid jug and a mug with the queen's head on it.

He was half rearing, and he had a broken stump on his shoulders.

"Excuse me," said the Sandmare, nosing the window. "Could you tell me where to find Polly?"

The glass horse narrowed his eyes. "Little Polly, you mean? Freckles? Curly mop? Big teeth?"

The Sandmare nodded eagerly.

"Why do you want to find her?" asked the glass horse.

"I hope she'll be able 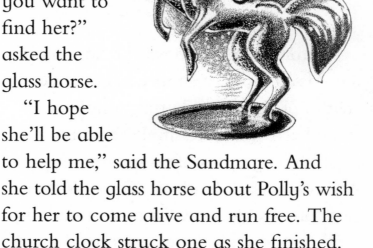 to help me," said the Sandmare. And she told the glass horse about Polly's wish for her to come alive and run free. The church clock struck one as she finished.

The glass horse nodded thoughtfully. "All very well to run, but where were you thinking of running to?"

"That's the trouble," said the Sandmare. "I only know that it has to be far away. I . . . I did think of going as far as the stars, but now I know that's silly. There isn't enough time for that."

"Hey, you run after your dreams," encouraged the glass horse. "Go for it. You might not get there, but you might not end up on the beach, either."

"But how will I get up there?" whinnied the Sandmare.

The glass horse sighed. "Probably have to fly. And wings aren't easy to come by." He peered ruefully at his broken shoulders. "I should know. Used to have wings myself."

"Goodness, I'm so sorry," murmured the Sandmare.

"Never mind me." The glass horse
perked up. "You're a drawing. All you
need is someone to draw you some
wings."

"Polly drew my tail," said the
Sandmare.

"Then she should be able to manage
wings," whinnied the glass horse. "She's
a clever girl."

"Do you know where she lives?" snuffled the Sandmare.

"I did," pondered the glass horse, waving his hoof. "Now, let me think. Polly's mother bought a rocking horse from here. A mean, moody old thing. Hope you don't run into him. Anyway, he kept boasting about where he was going. The Blacksmith's Arms. That was the name of the place. I think Polly must live there."

The Sandmare gave an excited whinny. "The Blacksmith's Arms?"

"I'd head uphill if I were you," said the glass horse. "I've watched her go that way."

"Thank you so much," said the Sandmare.

"You're welcome," the glass horse

called after her. "Just don't listen to *anyone* telling you to give up . . . And watch out for that rocking horse. His mood swings when he does. He can turn quite nasty."

THE ROCKING HORSE

"His mood swings when he does? What could the glass horse have meant by that?" the Sandmare wondered aloud. Still, it gave her something to think about as she dragged herself up the steep hill. Her legs seemed weaker than they used to be. They ached terribly. She didn't make it to the top of the hill until two o'clock. But she was in luck. The Blacksmith's Arms was right there.

No door was open, of course. "But all

the windows
are shut, too,"
puzzled the
Sandmare. "How
will I get in?"
Then she
spotted a tiny
door set within the front door. It was
really meant for a
cat. "Maybe if I make
myself very small . . ."

She curled up
tight, in the way you
might roll up a piece
of paper. Then she
launched her rolled
self at the cat door. It swung open far
too easily.

"Too fast," she
gasped as she bowled
across the hall. She
stuck tight under some
curved wooden struts.

"Now where am I?" She partly unfurled to look. Then she curled up like an armadillo. She had rolled straight under the rockers of the rocking horse.

"I see you," called a creaky voice. "Come out."

There was no point in hiding. She peeked her eyes and nose out. The rocking horse was facing straight ahead, so he seemed to look down his black-spotted nose at her.

"Hello there." He smiled pleasantly. "Now, what can you be doing under my rocker?"

"I . . . I came to find Polly," croaked the Sandmare, uncurling a little more.

41

In uncurling, she pressed against the rocker and tipped the rocking horse back a teeny bit.

"Have I got this right?" murmured the rocking horse. "Could you possibly be the sand drawing that Polly's been babbling on about?"

"Yes, that's me. Could you tell me where she is?" the Sandmare asked, uncurling further against the front rocker.

The rocking horse swung back even more. "I certainly will not tell you where she is," hissed the rocking horse, glaring at the ceiling. "Hasn't she done enough for you already?" He sounded very angry.

"I didn't think Polly would mind," the Sandmare said, unrolling completely to try to explain.

The rocking horse tipped almost over. "Mind?" he snarled. "*I* mind. I'm the house horse. I decide who sees Polly. AND I'VE DECIDED TO CRUSH YOU!"

Desperately the Sandmare strained to escape, but in her struggle she accidentally kicked the hall rug under the rocking horse's back rocker. Down swung the front rocker, pinning her on her back.

"Now he will do it." The Sandmare shuddered. "I'll be crushed sand in Polly's hallway."

The crunch didn't come. The rocker rested gently on her back.

"Let's be sensible." The rocking horse gazed down at her mildly. (He was tipped forward now.) "You can't see Polly in the middle of the night without a good reason."

The Sandmare trembled. She understood what the glass horse had meant now. "The rocking horse gets nasty only when he swings backward," she thought. "But how will I escape without tipping him again?"

"So?" asked the rocking horse. "Why do you want to see Polly?"

"I . . . want her to draw me some wings," gabbled the Sandmare. "I need them so I can fly to the stars, and I have to fly there before sunrise."

"Oh dear. You want to fly to the stars?" crooned the rocking horse. "You don't really believe in that, do you? And you seem so tired now. Yes, I think you may be beginning to crumble. It is almost morning."

"Maybe he's right," worried the Sandmare, as the church clock struck three. There did seem to be rather a lot of sand around her feet. But she thought of the glass horse. "I mustn't give up," she told herself. She kicked the rug out from the back rocker, and flung herself away from the front one. The rocking horse swung wildly.

CLONK!

"I'll squish you!" he snarled, his teeth snapping at the ceiling.

CLUNK!

"Be reasonable, my dear," he creaked, tipping forward again.

CLONK!

Somehow she'd spun toward his rear hooves. They were kicking toward her.

"Up here," piped a tiny voice.

The Sandmare leaped for the stairs.

There was a roar behind her. The rocking horse's rear hooves banged on the floor.

"Forget him," called the tiny voice. "Come up to the top, quick."

THE TOY HORSE

The Sandmare scissored up two flights of stairs. A fierce little pony on wheels was waiting for her, a yellow pony with blue spots, a proud puffed chest, and a bristle mane.

"I'm Biddle," he announced, whirring his wheels on the spot. "Hurry up. Come on in."

He bustled the Sandmare through a green door, and at last . . . there was Polly, kneeling up in bed, bouncing from side to side with excitement. The Sandmare felt so relieved and happy

that she couldn't even
speak, but that didn't
matter. Polly had plenty
to say.

"You took a long time,"
she said. "But we had a
feeling you'd come, so
Biddle watched for you.
You're quite safe now.
We'll look after you. You
can live in the wardrobe and . . ."

The Sandmare found her voice. "I
can't," she neighed. Miserably she told
Polly how little time was left, and how
she needed wings, and how it was
probably all too late anyway.

Polly looked very disappointed, but
she nodded bravely. Then she sat back
on her heels and said, "Never mind.
Don't you worry. We'll sort you out
somehow. Only . . . I'm not sure how to
draw your wings. You're not lying on
the sand anymore."

"I know where you can draw," Biddle said with a smirk. "Help me move the bed." He pushed his forehead against the bedpost. Polly scrambled to look.

"Oh, I see." She smiled. "Clever Biddle."

When the bed was in the middle of the room, Polly made the Sandmare lie down on the floor where the bed had been. The Sandmare didn't much want to. That bit of floor was thick with dust and fluff, and she could feel a sticky caramel wrapper prickling her tummy. She soon stopped minding. Polly was drawing wings in the dust above her shoulders.

"That's good drawing." Biddle nodded.

The Sandmare craned around to look, too. "Are they joined on to me?" she asked.

Polly smoothed the dust lines into the sand ones. "They are now." She wiped her hands. "Try standing up."

The Sandmare stood, and the dust
wings came, too.

"Yay!" cheered Biddle, revving his
wheels.

"But I can hardly feel them," worried
the Sandmare. "They aren't made of the
same stuff as the rest of me. They don't
seem very strong."

51

"They'll work just fine," said Polly, opening the window and sniffing the air. "But it's almost morning. You'd better get going."

"You're not allowed out there, Polly," warned Biddle.

"I'll watch from here," Polly said, helping the Sandmare through the window.

The Sandmare stumbled out onto the roof. She tried not to notice the sand that was billowing from her legs as she wobbled there.

"Go on," bossed Polly, looking at the sky. "It's time to go. I'll wish on a star for you." She picked out the brightest star, pointed at it, and squeezed her eyes shut. "There. It's done," she said. "Time to fly."

The Sandmare twitched her shoulders. The dust wings hardly moved. They didn't feel part of her at all. "But I've got this far," she told herself. "I can't give up now just because I feel tired." She planted her wobbly feet as firmly as she could, screwed up her eyes, and expected to fly.

"Try harder," encouraged Polly when nothing happened.

The Sandmare's ears drooped. "It's not working."

"Of course it is," said Polly. "I wished, didn't I? It worked yesterday."

"It did." The Sandmare nodded more bravely. She tried again.

After a bit, Biddle said, "Maybe the Sandmare is like an airplane. Maybe she needs a runway."

They all looked at the gentle slope of the roof.

"And I think," said Polly quietly, "for a good takeoff she'll need wheels."

"But I don't have wheels," said the Sandmare.

"Biddle does."

SANDMARE ON WHEELS

"No!" piped Biddle. "She's not having my wheels!"

"But you could give her a ride," pleaded Polly.

"She's too big!"

"Not on your back," explained Polly. "Look at your wheel platform. There's enough room for the Sandmare to put one hoof in front of you and one hoof behind you. Then, when you're going really fast, she'll take off."

"But I won't be able to see where I'm going," squawked Biddle furiously. "And how will I get home afterward?"

"I'll come and find you," said Polly.

"You're not allowed out on your own."

"No one'll know. I'll be very quick . . . Please, Biddle." Polly stroked Biddle's bristles. He liked being stroked. "It'll be all right," Polly pleaded.

The Sandmare wasn't so sure. There wasn't much room for her feet on that wheel platform. "It might not be safe," she mumbled.

"Are you saying my wheels aren't safe?" bellowed Biddle.

"No," the Sandmare protested. "But what if I don't fly? You'll get hurt if we crash."

"My wheels never crash," roared Biddle.

It was half-past four in the morning.

"Go on," wheedled Polly. "Wheel down the roof with Biddle, and flap your wings. When you're going fast enough . . . you'll take off."

The Sandmare looked up at

the stars. They were fading fast. It was almost dawn.

"Don't you think my wheels are good enough?" said Biddle, huffily hopping down onto the tiles. He swiveled his wheels to keep himself from rolling.

"Okay," the Sandmare decided. "I'll do it."

"Get on with it, then," said Biddle, wriggling.

Polly said, "Jump on and push with your back leg."

The Sandmare hobbled and hopped . . . and pushed and . . .

"Wheeeeee . . ." she whinnied as they zoomed along the roof.

"Hold your wings out to catch the wind," called Polly.

The Sandmare did. It was thrilling. Almost at the edge of the roof now, she stared ahead, ready to lift off . . . when she caught sight of the first flush of dawn. "I'm too late!" she wailed, and that was when everything went wrong.

Pandemonium!

The wind drove into her side as if she were a sail, and the wheel platform whooshed sideways. There was nothing Biddle could do. They were out of control.

BANG!

They jolted off the roof.

BUMP!

They landed on top of the bay window.
Sand crumbled from the Sandmare,
hitting Biddle full in the face.

"Fly, you dust bunny," he squealed as they plunged—

BASH! WALLOP!

—down onto the kitchen roof.

They were still rolling, but the Sandmare shook with despair. "I can't do it. It's no use . . ."

"Don't give up now, Sandmare," shouted Polly. "It's not too late. The sun isn't up yet."

But the Sandmare didn't hear. She was panicking too much to listen.

THUMP!

They smacked into the sandbox.

RUMBLE!

They tore down the path . . .

"You've got to steer away from the hill, Biddle," yelled Polly.

"I can't see where I'm steering,"
howled Biddle. "There's sand in my
eyes. Why did you let this lunatic near
my wheels?"

Polly shouted louder. "Come on,
Sandmare . . . You could still take off."

"Just flap, grit-head!" bawled Biddle.
"Or we'll smash to pieces."

Once again the wind slammed into the
Sandmare. They careered down the hill.

"I'm coming,
Biddle," Polly bellowed
after them. "I'll save you."

"She'll be too late!" The Sandmare
panicked as they hurtled toward the
pier.

"Can't you jump off or something?"
snarled Biddle. "We'll hit the merry-go-
round any minute."

"I'll stop somehow," gasped the
Sandmare. But she was too nervous to

try flying, and as more sand scattered away from her she found that she couldn't even move her weak legs now.

"Yuck! Can't you control that sand stuff?" spit Biddle.

THUD!
They hit the
wooden boards
of the pier.

"Got to save Biddle," said the Sandmare frantically. "Got to do something."

The merry-go-round loomed above them as she desperately threw her whole body sideways.

"Whoooaaa!" Biddle screamed. The wheel platform swerved, and they slammed to one side. They just missed the merry-go-round. "Now we're going to fall off the end of the pier," shouted Biddle. "And I don't think I'll float."

"HELP, SOMEBODY!" screeched the Sandmare.

Somebody heard. Out whisked a giant arm. Up in a gorilla hug went Biddle.

But a gust of wind blasted the Sandmare out from the gorilla's grasp. She was light as an autumn leaf now that so much sand had crumbled away. She tumbled along the pier, past the

cotton candy stands and the burger
booth, onward to the end of the pier.

"Slipped out of my hands," groaned
the gorilla. "She won't stop in time.
She'll be in the sea any minute. She's
had it."

"Wait,"
said Biddle.
"Look!"

THE FLYING HORSE

The Sandmare was blown into the
mouth of the giant slide. There must
have been wind in the tunnel, too. Up
she skidded, rocketing round the slippery
chute. Just as suddenly, the tunnel ended.
She shot outdoors, still on the chute.
More fresh air now, and a good view if
she wanted to look. The Sandmare
didn't want to look. "What happens
when I reach the top?" she whinnied.
"What happens then?"

She couldn't feel the wind behind her
anymore, couldn't work out why she
still spiraled upward. There was an odd

swishing sound just behind her ears.
From the corner of her eye she caught
sight of something moving. She turned
to look.

Her wings were flapping, carrying
her up the chute.

She was spinning around the last spiral now. Skimming the railings, shooting up, and up, her wings twisting like helicopter propellers. And she was light enough now for the dust wings to lift her into the sky. Flying at last. But even as she rejoiced, the first red rays of the sun crept over the hills. For a moment she glowed and twinkled in the light, then the last of her lines scattered into sand and dust.

"Too late," sighed the Sandmare. "It's

morning. Time to fall back to the sea."

But a dawn wind bundled the sand and dust upward. Of course, the pebble eye was too heavy. It dropped below. Without it, the Sandmare couldn't see anymore.

"But I can still think," she realized, as the whirlwind of sand rose into the sky. When the warm wind rolled higher, it cooled. Tiny drops of water coated all her dust and sand grains. And soon they were part of a fluffy, clingy mist.

The Sandmare didn't know that a cloud is made when teeny fragments of water and dust drift together in the sky. But what was left of her began to understand something, as she floated over the land and up toward the brightness. "I'm still chasing a star!" she realized. And she spoke the truth. For the sun is the nearest star of all.

Polly reached the pier, out of breath, just as PER-CLATTER, a brown pebble fell from the sky, bounced once, and rolled to her feet. Polly picked it up. She had held it before.

"It's the Sandmare's eye," she whispered.

"So the wings didn't work," croaked Biddle.

But the gorilla wasn't so sure. "It might be something she didn't need anymore," he said.

A pink cloud, like a piece of pulled cotton candy, drifted over the sun. Polly had seen that sort of cloud before. She knew the name of it. "A mare's tail cloud." She smiled.

This is how the long-drawn-out strokes of cloud looked:

"That cloud looks awfully familiar," Biddle said. "Just like one of your drawings."

"I think so too." Polly grinned, rolling the pebble in her hand.